Ramu
a story of India

Ramu
a story of India

by RAMA MEHTA

Foreword by Santha Rama Rau
Illustrated by W. T. Mars

ANGUS & ROBERTSON
London   Sydney   Melbourne

First published in the United Kingdom in 1968 by

ANGUS & ROBERTSON LTD

54 Bartholomew Close, London
89 Castlereagh Street, Sydney
107 Elizabeth Street, Melbourne

First published in the United States in 1966 by McGraw-Hill, Inc.:

Printed in Great Britain
by Morrison and Gibb Limited, London and Edinburgh

contents

In finalizing this story, I have been greatly assisted by Leigh Dean who has been most patient and helpful in carefully going through the manuscript and bringing it to its present shape.

list of Indian words

their meaning and pronunciation

Anna *(an-na)*	Sixteen annas to a rupee; 7.5 rupees to U.S. dollar (The anna is no longer in the Indian currency)
Babu *(bah-bu)*	A term of respect used when addressing a merchant
Babuji *(bah-bu-gee)*	A term of respect
Bapuji *(bah-pu-gee)*	Honoured father
Beta *(bay-thah)*	Son
Bhaiya *(bh-ai-yah)*	Brother
Bibi *(bee-bee)*	Senior wife or woman in the house
Brinjal *(brinj-al)*	Eggplant
Charpai *(char-paii)*	A four-legged wooden frame that can be made into a cot
Choli *(cho-lee)*	Close-fitting bodice worn under the sari
Chop-wala *(chop-vwala)*	A man who makes potato cakes
Chowkidar *(cho-kee-dar)*	A watchman
Churi-wala *(choori-vwala)*	A man who sells toys and glass bangles
Churi-wali *(choori-vwalee)*	A woman who sells toys, beads, and bangles
Dada *(dah-dah)*	Elder one, indicating a friend or relative
Dal *(daal)*	A lentil
Diwali *(Di-vwali)*	The Festival of Lights
Dhoti *(dho-thi)*	A straight piece of cloth that men wrap around their waists, drawing the loose end between their legs and tucking it into the waistband
Ghee *(ghee)*	Melted butter
Gram *(gram)*	Roasted edible seed, a form of lentil
Gulli *(gal-lee)*	A narrow lane
Halwa *(hal-vwa)*	Sweets
Halwai *(hal-vwa-ee)*	One who makes sweets
Hathi-pol *(ha-thee-pol)*	The Elephant Gate
Haveli *(ha-ve-lee)*	An ancestral house
Ji *(gee)*	A suffix added to the name of an older person and to proper names to show respect
Katha *(kat-tha)*	The base for pan (*see* Pan)

Kohl *(call)*	An eye black worn on the outside rim of the eye; a medicine as well as a cosmetic
Kum-kum *(kum-kum)*	A red powder
Lakshmi *(Lucks-mee)*	The Goddess of Wealth
Ma *(mah)*	An endearing term for any 'mother'
Maharana *(Ma-ha-rah-na)*	Long ago the royal family of Udaipur was called Maharaja. The military sect was called Maharana. As time passed, the Maharana ran the city-state. Today Udaipur has a Maharana but no Maharaja
Mahout *(mah-hoot)*	An elephant trainer
Mela *(may-lah)*	A fair
Neem *(neem)*	The twig of a tree used for cleaning teeth and for antiseptic purposes. It has a lemony-bitter taste but leaves the mouth feeling wonderfully cool and refreshed
Om *(ohm)*	A sacred Hindu symbol meaning peace. It looks like two interlocking triangles
Pan *(pan)*	A green, heart-shaped, edible leaf chewed after meals
Pan-wala *(pan-vwala)*	One who sells pan
Puree *(poo-ree)*	A round wheat pancake which puffs up when fried
Puree-wala *(poo-ree-vwala)*	A man who makes purees
Ricksha *(rick-shaw)*	A three-wheeled carriage built in a bicycle frame
Ricksha-wala *(rick-shaw-vwala)*	A male rickshaw driver
Roti *(roh-tee)*	A baked wheat pancake used as bread
Rupee *(roo-pee)*	An Indian coin (*see* Anna)
Sagar *(sah-gur)*	A man-made lake
Sahib *(sah-hib)*	Sir
Saraswati *(Sa-ras-wa-tee)*	The Goddess of Knowledge
Sari *(sah-ree)*	Always six straight yards of cloth, silk, or cotton, which the women drape around themselves to make a dress
Thalli *(tha-lee)*	A round metal plate used for eating
Tonga *(tongah)*	A horse-drawn carriage
Tonga-wala *(tongah-vwala)*	A male driver of a horse-drawn carriage

Note: *It is difficult to express in the English language the exact pronunciation of Indian words, as there are many sounds which do not exist in English. The pronunciation indicated is as accurate a transcription as is available.*

foreword

I do not recall a modern Indian children's book that captures with such authenticity and charm the atmosphere of a small Indian town and the childhood drama that exists within it.

Mrs Rama Mehta conveys the feeling of an Indian family, its ties, loyalties, duties, wonders, and excitements. Perhaps without even knowing it, she gives a picture of day-to-day Indian life that is both moving and true. It may be wrong to call this a 'children's book' in a conventional sense, for the reaches of her experience and understanding should be savoured by adults as well.

In this story of a young boy and his ambitions and experiences over a short time, a new (or old) picture of India emerges that reveals far more about the people, the living, and the country than have many heavier tomes. One sees, at last, that though India may offer her people a poor living, it offers them a rich life.

Santha Rama Rau

the dream

A pale moon slipped from the cover of a cloud and shone down on the ancient city of Udaipur. It lay within the boundaries of a crumbling wall which had surrounded it for hundreds of years. Only one building rose above the clutter of whitewashed houses. That was the great Jagdish Temple, whose spires were closest to heaven.

In one of the small mud-plastered houses, a boy slept on the kitchen floor with a blanket drawn over his face. His name was Ramu. As he tossed and turned on the straw mat, deep in sleep, he dreamed it was Diwali. Everywhere people were rejoicing and preparing to welcome the Goddess of Wealth. Today she would come down to earth to give her blessings, and every deserving person would receive a gift. Ramu wished for only one thing—the beautiful red and gold mouth organ that hung on a peg in Tulsi's shop.

He dreamed that he was with his friends, Ajit and Chotu, and that they were all laughing and skipping down the narrow, dingy gullis, through the bustling bazaar, hurrying toward the Elephant Gate to watch the Maharana enter the city. Ramu tried to keep up with his friends, but the harder he tried, the slower he seemed to go. He was about to give up when, dancing in the air just beyond his reach, was his mouth organ. Sometimes it sped ahead, making him race to keep it in sight. Sometimes it hung motionless, too high for him to touch. Around and around in circles it led him, and finally it slowed behind the huge painted hindquarters of a royal elephant, the last in the Maharana's procession. As the long line of elephants plodded, their footfalls sent up thick puffs of dust, making Ramu hold his breath as he tried to catch the mouth organ. He followed the royal procession out of the city and through tall, steel-spiked gates into the inner courtyard of the palace. Here there was great celebrating with music and dancing and singing.

Suddenly, in his dream, the music and singing stopped, and from afar echoed the notes of a trumpet. The mouth organ, heading toward the sound, darted into a maze of corridors. Ramu went after it, his path lit by small oil lamps. And as he passed over the marble tiles, rows of guards in flowing velvet robes and drawn steel swords stood at attention.

At a mighty pair of carved doors, the mouth organ stopped, then vanished. Ramu stopped. Courtiers bowed low and opened the doors for him to pass.

Ramu entered a great hall and fell to his knees. Before him sat the Maharana on his throne of gold, dressed in a white jeweled coat. Four men stood behind the Maharana, fanning him with horsehair switches. Six men in gold and red livery stood beside him with naked swords.

And over the throne was spread a large embroidered canopy supported by four poles of silver and gold.

Never in his life had Ramu seen such a sight. He could neither move nor speak, but the Maharana seemed to know him. He smiled and beckoned him forward. Ramu obeyed and slowly crawled across the thick carpets that covered the marble floor. When he reached the throne, the Maharana held out his glittering hand. Ramu's eyes grew wide. There, brighter than any jewel, was his red and gold mouth organ.

A cry of surprise burst from Ramu's lips, startling him awake. He opened his eyes. His mother was on the floor next to him, stroking his forehead. Softly she was saying, 'Hush, beta, I'm here beside you. Do not be afraid. It is just a dream.'

Still in his other world, Ramu moved closer to his mother's warmth and looked around the kitchen. Somewhere outside he heard the howling of a jackal. Was it possible it had only been a dream? It must have been, he thought, for everything in the room looked just the same. There was the unlit fireplace, and the pots and pans and thallis were stacked on the dried cow-dung floor. The large earthenware water pots were also in their place beside the low, ink-stained table. It must still be early, thought Ramu, for no sound came from his sisters' tiny room nor from the room of his father.

As Ramu's mother went to light the fire, he got to his feet, rolled up his straw mat and blanket, and put them on the shelf above the fireplace. He splashed his face with cold water and went out to the open shed in the courtyard to embrace his cow and her calf. Ramu had no toys, so they had become his special playthings. And the cow was very useful, for she gave them all the milk they needed.

Ramu milked the cow and told her of his dream and the fabulous palace he had visited. As he finished, he heard his father calling.

'Ramu, you must hurry. School does not wait for you.'

Ramu's father, Kalu Ram, was a tall man with strong muscles which he needed in his work. He was a halwai, a maker of sweets, as his father and grandfather had been. Kalu Ram had learned to make the fancy sweets when he was still a boy. His shop was small and plain, and everyone respected him and he was proud of his profession.

But there was one thing that did not please Kalu Ram—he did not know how to read and write. And he wanted his son, Ramu, to know these things.

'Just wait,' Kalu Ram would tell his wife, 'until Ramu becomes the first boy in our community to have passed school.' His eyes would begin to shine with pride. 'He will one day be the best halwai in the city of Udaipur.'

Ramu's mother did not understand all the virtues of education. She worried more about the marriage dowries Ramu's younger sisters, Munni and Ganga, would some day need. If Ramu went to work in his father's shop, he could help to earn the money for their dowries.

Ramu brought the brass bucket of milk into his house. Then he washed himself and sat down on the floor to eat his morning meal. Today, more than ever before, he did not want to go to school. He remembered the days when he had been his own master—free to roam the busy market-place and to chat with the men, to play marbles in the streets, and to watch the cars honking and inching their way through the crowds. Once he had even ridden atop a small red Ford. And there were the visits to the bazaar to buy things for his mother. Ramu enjoyed the tricky game of bargaining, and he often got extra oil poured into his container. Even taking care of his two sisters had been more fun than going to school.

'You are late this morning, Ramu,' prodded his mother. 'You cannot dream all night and all day, too. Ajit and Chotu must have gone off without you.'

Ramu finished his piece of roti, slowly swallowed the last of his milk, and went to get his books.

'Here is the four-anna you wanted for the notebook,' said his mother.

Ramu thanked her and hurried out of his house. As he passed the grand haveli next door, the owner, who was a rich palace official, waved and offered Ramu a ride in his fine car.

'My friends are waiting for me at the crossroads,' called Ramu, and thanked his honoured friend.

He ran through the many tiny, open-drained gullis and arrived breathless at the point where the two paved roads crossed in the middle of the city. Here, every morning, he met his classmates, Ajit and Chotu, and together they walked to school.

'Hurry up,' shouted Ajit as Ramu flopped to the ground.

'Next time you can walk to school alone,' grumbled Chotu.

Tucking their books under their arms, the three bare-footed boys started off, taking long strides to make up for lost time. As they walked, Ajit and Chotu threw fistfuls of gram seed into their mouths. Ramu went along in silence, thinking about his dream.

The boys moved briskly on, their shirts half tucked into their khaki pants. Winter had set in and the cold mornings made their eyes and noses run, but they preferred the nip of the cold wind to the winds of the warmer months that made them sweat.

The streets were quiet in the early morning. As they passed through the bazaar, Ramu lagged behind and watched his other playmates who did not go to school. Some were setting out the day's vegetables, others were carrying brick loads, and still others were working in their fathers' shops. They seemed to be so much better off than he, who got no pay for going to school. It was then that Ramu got an idea. It was the day of the Mangal Mela and that was no time to be shut up in school.

'Listen, boys,' he began, but his two friends had already run to the cows who were wandering from one rubbish pile to another, smelling and munching what they liked.

Ajit crept up behind a cow and grabbed her tail.

The cow mooed loudly and Ramu and Chotu looked

around in alarm to be sure that no one had seen Ajit.

'What do you think you are doing?' whispered Chotu. 'Do you want us all to get into trouble?'

Ajit laughed and led the way across the moat under Hathi-pol, the giant Elephant Gate to the north. They walked along the country road that curved for a mile to the right and soon reached the path that led to school. Ajit and Chotu quickened their pace, but Ramu paused.

'Come on,' called his friends, 'we must run or we shall be late. There goes the first bell.'

'I don't think I am going,' said Ramu. Ajit and Chotu stopped and stared at him. 'I would much rather be at the mela at Lake Fateh Sagar,' he added.

Ajit and Chotu looked hard at their friend.

'It would never do, Ramu,' said Chotu. 'It is not worth all the trouble it will get you into.'

'Besides,' said Ajit, 'the festival of Diwali is not far off, and we can have much more fun then. Are you coming?'

Ramu shook his head. 'No,' he answered. He had already made up his mind, and he did not move as his classmates ran off down the path.

'Study hard!' he shouted. But Ajit and Chotu did not look back and disappeared into the schoolyard.

at the mela

Ramu's heart felt light and gay as he stood in the bright morning sun planning the shortest way to the lake. First, he would have to take the asphalt road across to the other side of town. The road was fast and led right to the Stadium Parade Grounds. So early in the day the guards would not be about. He could cut through the grounds, go up the hill, pass the State Guest House at the top, and run down the other side to Lake Pichola.

In the distance, Ramu heard the jingle of anklet bells and the singing of carefree workers as they hurried on their way to the city. Then the ringing of the final school bell echoed over the fields. For just a moment, Ramu wanted to run and join his classmates. But a voice cut through his thoughts.

'Ramu. Eh, Ramu. How is it you are standing here? Is today a holiday from school?' Ramu spun around. It was only Mithoo, the ricksha-wala, who had stopped across the road.

Ramu's face flushed with guilt as he answered, 'It is not your business. You are not my ... '

Mithoo laughed. 'Ah, it is like that. You are taking a small holiday. As for me, I never could understand why you were sent to school. I never went, nor did my father or his father. I am waiting to see what good all this education does you,' he added with a wink.

Ramu felt a little better.

'Anyway,' asked Mithoo as he got ready to pedal off, 'where are you going?'

'To the fair at the lake,' replied Ramu.

'Come on then, hop in. At this early hour, customers are few.'

Ramu felt the four-anna coin in his pocket.

'How much will you take, dada?'

'Nothing, of course. Imagine taking money from a child,' said Mithoo, a little hurt. 'Come on, jump in and don't make such a fuss next time.'

Ramu jumped into the buggy which was attached to the cycle. The seat, stuffed with coconut fibre, was comfortable, and Ramu slid back and relaxed. Sitting all alone, he felt like a prince being driven by his coachman. If only his friends could see him now, thought Ramu, wouldn't they be envious! Mithoo pedalled fast, and the cold wind which hit Ramu in the face made his eyes water. He felt so happy he wanted to sing.

'Ramu,' called the ricksha-wala over his shoulder, 'tell me what you learn in school. Is it really difficult to read and write?'

'Dada, we learn about the coming of the British sahibs and how they took over the whole of India. And we learn about the great kings of Rajasthan—about all the rivers there are in India. But what is really hard is to read and write English. This, I can tell you, takes brains.'

'But what good is it to know English?' said Mithoo. 'I know your type who go to school because your fathers think it is the smart thing to do these days. I'm sure none of you boys can keep accounts as well as I do. Let anyone try to cheat me, and he'll soon see.'

On they rode through the parade grounds and up the hill. Mithoo was out of breath but he was still pedalling. When he had his normal load he walked beside the ricksha, pulling it until he reached the flat road again.

From the crest of the hill Ramu saw the Maharana's palace, the shimmering waters of Fateh Sagar Lake, and the mela spread out before him on the banks of the lake. All along the embankment washermen were unloading great wicker baskets full of laundry from their donkeys. Some had already begun beating the clothes against the large flat stones at the water's edge. Ramu could hear the slap of cloth against stone.

When the ricksha reached the bottom of the hill, Mithoo put one foot down and brought the cycle to a halt.

'Here we are!' he called. 'Now have fun!'

Ramu jumped out of the ricksha and looked up at Mithoo in gratitude. No one had ever given him such a fine ride. 'Thank you, Mithoo, dada,' he said at last. 'I hope you have luck ... ' But Mithoo was already off with his first client—a nice, fat man with a turban.

The mela grounds were shaded by big mango trees

whose branches were heavy with thick clusters of deep green leaves. As crowds poured in, men were putting the last touches to their stalls and digging fire pits for the roasting of peanuts and gram.

Ramu was wondering where to begin when his eyes fell on the potato chop-wala as he sat on his haunches before a big metal plate. The jolly man was dressed in a dhoti and he was putting all his strength into squeezing and mashing the cooked potatoes. Two little boys helped him by throwing the hot, peeled potatoes into the big plate. Ramu went and sat beside the chop-wala, his mouth watering at the thought of the hot, fried potato cakes. On one side of the metal plate was a large pot of sour tamarind sauce, and on the other were tins full of spices. Ramu leaned forward to warm his hands over the open fire. He was about to be rash and place an order when the man raised his head and said, 'Little fellow, wouldn't you like to taste my first cake?' The chop-wala took a lump of dough and, patting it round with his palms, threw it into the sizzling pan which stood over the fire. Ramu watched the hot potato cake hungrily and reached out to touch it.

'Now wait, don't be in such a hurry,' cautioned the chop-wala. 'The spices must be added, and in the right amount. Let no one say that Laloo does not know his job!' He poured a spoonful of the dark brown tamarind sauce over the cake and with his fingers added a pinch of spice from each tin. When the cake was ready, the chop-wala put it in a cup of dried leaves, pinned the leaves together with small sticks, and handed it to Ramu. Ramu smacked his lips as he put the cup to his mouth.

'Now tell me, little fellow, aren't Laloo's cakes the best you have ever tasted?' asked the chop-wala.

'Oh, dada, they are delicious,' murmured Ramu as he licked the cup to get the last bit of sauce.

'Now you know what name to give when people ask who makes the best potato cakes.' Before Ramu could reply, the chop-wala was busy serving a family of five.

Ramu's heartbeat quickened, for now the grounds swarmed with people of every shape and size. The air vibrated with the shrill whistles of bamboo, paper, and tin. A man with a pole filled with toys was shouting, 'Come, sirs, one and all, see how this bird sings and eats.' As he kept repeating these words, he pulled the strings of a wooden bird, making it peck.

'How about a jumping frog or a monkey or a balloon?' he asked as he caught Ramu's eye. 'Only four annas.'

Ramu smiled and quickly turned away. He was not in a hurry to spend his money. He wanted to see everything first. Besides, the feel of the round coin lying safely in his pocket made him happy.

On the far side of the grounds, Ramu came to a sudden stop. Before him lay a glittering array of clay toys. Kings and queens stood in regal splendor. Soldiers were lined up in full uniform, with gold turbans and orange tunics and strings of pearls hanging from their necks.

Ramu picked up a king atop an elephant and began examining it.

'What do you mean by touching my toys?' snapped a voice.

Ramu dropped the king as if he had been slapped. He saw a withered old woman huddled in a corner sniffing snuff and watching him through half-closed eyes.

'Don't you know I am from Kailashpuri Village,' the woman went on, 'and that my toys are famous in the court of the Maharana of Udaipur?'

'Ma,' stammered Ramu, 'I was only looking to see which one to buy. They are all so lovely.'

'Hai-e-e, you don't know which one to buy, eh? You think you can fool me. I, who have served the Maharana

of Udaipur for the last fifty years, can judge people. I know smart types like you.' She stopped to clear her throat. Ramu, seeing his chance, quickly slipped away. He didn't dare look back lest he see those eyes glaring at him.

From nearby, Ramu heard the creaking sound of the giant wooden wheel. At the base stood a man, taking deep breaths and swinging the large handle that turned the ponderous wheel round and round. 'Faster, push faster!' shouted the children who sat in the wooden seats in pairs, and held on tightly to the bars. Slowly they glided off the ground. Then up, up into the air they rocketed, squealing loudly with joy and fright.

Ramu watched carefully as a short, stubby man collected two annas from each child in the moving line. He waited until the man's back was turned. In a flash, he slid in at the head of the line and jumped into one of the empty seats. He gripped the bar as the wheel, whining and groaning, sent him out into space. Sitting on top of the world, Ramu laughed and shouted with the others, 'Faster! Faster!'

When the wheel finally slowed down and came to a stop, two large hands grabbed Ramu's neck. The wheel had stopped right in front of the man who was collecting the money.

'You think I didn't see you jump in, you little rascal! No one in the city of Udaipur can fool Kali!' The stubby man gave Ramu's neck a twist. Ramu dug the four-anna out of his pocket and held out his open hand. Kali took the coin, threw it into the air, and saw the sun dance and sparkle off it.

'Yes, it is a good coin all right,' said Kali with a twinkle in his eyes, but one hand still held Ramu's neck.

Down the line the children were growing impatient with the delay and had started clapping their hands and stamping their feet. In the confusion, Ramu felt the hand loosen its grip on his neck and he broke free.

'Here, wait. Come back,' called Kali. 'Take your coin and remember it is a good one, too.' Gratefully, Ramu pocketed his precious four annas, then ran from Kali and the wooden wheel as fast as possible.

The shock and relief of having his money returned put a sudden empty, hungry feeling in Ramu's stomach. Food stalls were everywhere and he was headed for the nearest one when a small child in front of him started to howl, 'My violin strings are broken. I want a new one. Buy me a new one.' With that, the child threw down his fine clay violin and disappeared with his father into the crowds.

Before it could get trampled under the passing feet, Ramu bent and picked it up. His hands went over the bowl and along the rod: nothing was cracked. Only one string had snapped and lay curled at the base of the rod. And one string was very easy to fix.

Ramu's eyes filled with joy as he gently fingered the clay violin. It would have cost him at least four annas— this he was sure of. The thought of all the pleasant hours he would spend playing the many tunes he knew and amusing his two small sisters filled his heart with music and seemed to help him push his way through the crush of people. The smell of purees coming out fresh and hot from the nearby puree-wala's pan made Ramu's mouth water, and he squeezed even harder past legs and hips and stomachs until he reached the counter.

'Could I please have four purees for one anna?' No one heard him or bothered with his small order. There were people ordering purees by the dozens. Children and grownups were stuffing two purees into their mouths at a time and making loud smacking sounds with their lips.

'Please, may I have four purees,' said Ramu, this time in a louder voice. His stomach had begun to growl and he was growing impatient.

'Wait your turn,' replied the puree-wala. 'Can't you see I am serving this honoured sahib?'

To Ramu it seemed that this sahib was having his hundredth puree. His children were also clamouring for more. At this rate, Ramu thought, my chance will never come. He tried to turn around and leave, but instead he knocked over a cup of sauce. Just then, Ramu spotted the face of Ganesh, one of his gulli friends, who was working behind the counter.

'Ramu,' whispered Ganesh, 'come here.' In a second, Ramu was at the end of the counter where Ganesh sat cross-legged, busily pinning dried leaves together. Pretending not to know his friend, Ganesh quickly handed

Ramu a cup full of purees and another cup splashing with sauce. The boss saw the second cup being slipped under the counter.

'You boys are no good,' he shouted from the far end. 'I don't know why I keep chaps like you. You are neglecting the rich sahibs of the town by wasting your time on a small fellow with no money.'

Ganesh bent his head innocently and with skilful fingers began pinning the leaves as fast as he could. Ramu gave his friend a nod of thanks, then quietly made his way to a mango tree and stood leaning against the trunk eating his small purees dripping with delicious pepperwater.

Evening was falling fast now and Ramu could feel the tiredness creep up his legs. Many people were already starting home. The cries of the ricksha-walas and tonga-walas for clients caused a great commotion.

Ramu wished Mithoo would suddenly appear and give him another ride. The sooner he got home, the sooner he could repair the violin string and give a surprise concert after supper. He imagined the happy giggles and clapping of his sisters, Munni and Ganga, and the proud smiles of his father and mother. Ramu began to whistle.

'Little boy. Little boy with the whistle, come here.'

Ramu froze. There was something frightening and familiar about that voice. He turned around and his heart sank. The small, shrivelled-up woman sat with her toys piled high in a basket, sniffing the fine powder from the open snuffbox in her hands.

27

'Come here,' she called as she held Ramu's gaze.
'Come and help an old woman lift her basket.'

Without saying a word, Ramu went and helped raise
the basket on to the old woman's head.

'Here, little boy, don't be afraid. I saved these toys
for you—the king that you like and the queen. And don't
forget the horse—it is the best you will ever have. It is
Chetaka, the brave horse that died saving his master. Only
my son can make a horse like this.'

Ramu could not believe his eyes. He stared first at
the king and then at the queen and the horse. 'Ma, I have
only four annas. I cannot buy them all.'

The old woman laughed and her eyes screwed up in a
funny way, making her wrinkles knot together.

'You silly boy. You want to pay your grandmother
for things she is giving you? Where did you learn that?
Now, don't waste time. The basket grows heavy and I wish
to reach home before it is too dark. Be on your way.'

'Thank you, ma.' Ramu felt giddy with happiness,
as he marvelled over the toys and caressed them. Then he
untied the turban on his head and carefully wrapped the
toys in it. He made a tight knot so they would not rattle
and slung the bundle over his shoulder.

It was then that Ramu felt a sudden chill. The mela
grounds had emptied. All that remained were pieces of
paper, bits of broken earthenware cups and the pinned wet
leaves. Ramu knew it must be late, too late for his home-
coming to be a joyful one.

homecoming

Ramu moved swiftly through the deserted mango grove. The trees stood out against the dark which in winter creeps in quickly. Only a few minutes ago the trees seemed alive and happy, but now they made Ramu feel like running away from them. He jumped over a puddle and ran along a stream that lay between two roads. When the stream became narrow and muddy, he walked through it. His

ankles were covered with mud and his feet felt cold. He stamped his feet several times on the dry ground, then took the short cut home.

The dim street lights were on in the town of Udaipur, and a policeman stood at the point where several roads met. He was trying to direct the bullock carts, horse-buggies, motor cars, and cycle rickshas. But his whistle could hardly be heard above the honking, bell-ringing, and shouts of the impatient, tired travellers. Ramu crossed the street without waiting for a signal, dodged a few cars, and safely reached the other side. The distance from the town to the city seemed shorter tonight and soon he found himself passing under Hathi-pol, the Gate of the Elephants. Through this gate warriors once marched their elephants loaded with spears and guns to protect the city from invaders. Now the villagers used this ancient gateway. They tried to reach their homes in the country before darkness fell. Singing as they filed along one by one, the women carried their baskets of unsold vegetables on their heads. Some held their babies in their arms. A few children, shivering in the cold, followed the trail, trying to keep up with the elders.

Ramu knew most of the village folk, and often went to the open vegetable market to buy supplies for his mother.

As Ramu hurried on, he heard a woman call to him from the other side of the Elephant Gate.

'Ramu! Why haven't I seen you for such a long time? I hope all goes well with your family.' She stopped as she tucked her skirt a little higher. 'Tell your mother I am bringing fresh cucumbers into the market tomorrow. If she wants any, tell her to come bright and early.' Ramu nodded. The woman looked at his serious face and patted it. She pulled out a bunch of juicy radishes and gave it to him. Taking them, Ramu continued on his way and soon reached the broken-down wall surrounding the old city. A band of grass cutters were struggling along as they balanced stacks of grass on their heads. As they passed Ramu, he pulled out a few dry roots from a stack and put them in his mouth. The lighting of the narrow streets was poor and the road was rough and dusty. Oil lamps flickered from the lattice windows, and rings of smoke escaped from rooftops.

As Ramu approached his home, his heart began to pound. Why hadn't he been more careful about the time? What would he tell his father?

At the corner of the dimly-lit gulli next to his house stood a temple with its small pinnacle painted red and gold. Ramu climbed the uneven stone steps of the shrine and stood before the open temple door facing the beautiful image of the Goddess Lakshmi. Her hands were raised in Protection. Ramu folded his hands in respect, closed his eyes, and prayed.

'Mother of All, make me a good boy and forgive all my mistakes. Mother, Giver of All, don't let my father scold me for missing school. I promise never to do it again. Bless my parents and sisters.'

Then he went down on both knees and touched his head on the stone floor. As he lifted his eyes to the Goddess Lakshmi, her smile seemed sweet and her face gentle. Ramu felt much better. Now he jumped to ring the temple bell, missed, but tried again. The second time, the bell rang, filling the air with its shrill sound. The priest, who was turning his beads and repeating the names of gods and goddesses, stopped to bring him the holy water and the blessed sweets. Ramu took the holy water in the cup of his hands and drank it. He then accepted the handful of temple sugar balls, bowed his head in respect, and left. Before the first sugar ball had melted in his mouth, Ramu was at the doorstep of his house.

He lingered in front of the cracked wooden door, straightening his hair. He stuffed the toys under his shirt and tightened his belt. Then he knocked gently. He heard the rattle of the chain from inside as it fell from its clasp. Ramu waited, his hand holding the radishes.

The door swung open.

'Ramu!' His mother's face held fear and anger. 'Where have you been all day? Your father has gone to Chotu's house and I have been praying all evening, thinking something terrible has happened to you. Where have you been, you little devil?' With this, she pulled Ramu into the half-dark room where only a small lamp burned.

'I have brought you some radishes, ma.'

His mother did not answer as her eyes fell on the bundle bulging under his shirt.

'What are you hiding there, Ramu?'

'I did not go to school today, ma.'

'You wait and see what you get from your father when he finds out.' Saying this, she gave him a sharp slap on his cold cheek. 'This is what you do when your father works from morning to evening so you can go to school. He tries to save and won't eat fruit; he wants his son to be a big man.'

Ramu's eyes filled with tears. As he put down the radishes, he heard footsteps in the street, followed by knocking on the door. To Ramu it sounded like thunder. His mother hurriedly covered her head with her sari, pulled it a little over her face, and went to the door. Kalu Ram entered the house. He looked at his son gravely. 'So here you are,' he said. 'I have been everywhere. Chotu said he didn't know where you were. Ajit said he saw you in the morning.'

Ramu went quickly to his father and touched his feet, as was the custom.

'No, don't touch my feet, Ramu. You are not worthy of the trust I placed in you.'

Ramu felt hurt. A pain went through his chest as he rose without having paid his respects to his father.

'Where did you go, Ramu?' His father's face was tight with anger.

'I went to the mela, father,' stammered Ramu as he stood straight.

'With whose permission did you go there?'

There was silence.

'Don't you see, Ramu, sending you to school is not easy for us. Your mother hasn't bought a new sari in the last twelve months because she wants you to have good clothes for school. She saves in every way so that you can have all the books you need. And you think it is fun to

miss school.' His voice was heavy and sad and the words came slowly. 'I could easily make you work, but then you will go no farther than I have. I can't force you to study, but if you miss school again and go off on your own, that will be the last day of your school life.'

Ramu stood still, tears rolling down his cheeks.

'You can't pretend to be a rich boy and I can't pretend to be a rich man,' said Kalu Ram.

Ramu could stand it no longer. He sank down and caught hold of his father's feet. 'Father,' he said between sobs, 'I will never miss school again. Never, father. Please forgive me,' he begged with his head buried in his hands.

Kalu Ram drew his son up tenderly, and now his voice was gentle. 'Knowledge is to be respected. Otherwise, the Goddess of Knowledge will not bless you, my son. She is to be worshiped, which means you must show respect for those who do her work. Her blessings are very important to you. You will have to be punished for this disrespect.'

'Yes, father,' said Ramu as he wiped his eyes. 'I will pray to her to forgive me for today.'

Ramu's mother stood in the corner of the room. Ramu went to her and saw that she, too, was wiping tears with the end of her sari. He wanted to comfort her but his father said, 'It is already dark and we have not yet washed our hands and feet. Come, let us get ready for supper.'

As they began their evening meal, the air filled with the ringing of bells. The temple doors were closing for the night, for the gods and goddesses must also rest.

It was a quiet meal. When they had finished and the dishes were cleaned and stacked, Ramu for the first time waited eagerly for the ritual that brought him close to his mother. This night he made no excuses and sat still while his mother soaked her fingers in the little steel cup of oil and vigorously massaged the oil into his head. He even enjoyed the feeling as his scalp grew warm with the rubbing.

'Thank you, ma,' he said.

His mother looked into the serious eyes of her son. 'Ramu, beta, you are growing up too fast,' she said, and she hugged him tightly.

school

Next morning, Saturday, Ramu was up earlier than usual and sat out on the doorstep cleaning his teeth. He chewed the neem stick to pulp, spat in the drain, and tried to think how he could please his mother. Usually his mother was the first up, for she would clean the kitchen, fetch the water, and light the fire for the morning meal. But today Ramu wanted to do something special for her. The morning breeze and the twig's bitter juice cleared away the heaviness his sadness had brought. Now Ramu knew what he would do.

He had just gone to the shed to select some fine logs when he heard his mother's voice. 'Ramu, what are you doing up so early?'

Ramu paid no attention to her and carried in the logs.

'You should not be doing this,' she said as she sat down to light the fire. 'These are the days for you to read and write. Later on you can do all this.'

'Ma, let me light the fire,' he said in a whisper. His father and sisters were still sleeping.

Ramu stuffed newspaper underneath the clay fireplace and put dried twigs on top. Then he carefully arranged the heavy logs so there would be enough room for them to draw the breeze. When the paper burned out, he used the wooden pipe to blow air on the sparks to make the twigs flare up. Soon the flames rose high and the logs began to glow.

'You did that quickly,' said his mother. 'I always get the smoke into my eyes, especially now that the wood is wet.'

The vegetables were cut and prepared and the lentils had already been put into the water. The big pot was soon boiling. Ramu's mother was kneading the wheat flour with her hands to make the dough for the roti. 'Today, with your help, I will be through my work in a few minutes.'

Ramu sat in a corner, trying to learn the difficult English verbs. His sisters were tossing and turning in their room, a sign that they would soon be up.

'Come, Ramu,' said his mother, 'sit down and have your food. You must not be late for school.'

Ramu sat beside the fire while his mother gave him hot rotis spread with melted butter. Everything tasted so good today—he had two helpings of vegetables and even a second helping of the lentil soup which he did not usually like. Ramu ate so quickly that his mother could not roll out the rotis fast enough. She smiled as she watched her son.

Having eaten his fill and cleaned his plate with the ashes from the fireplace, he went into the storeroom where he kept his things and took out his school pants. He found a new, clean shirt on the trunk. He dressed and combed his hair, then picked up his schoolbag and went into his father's room. Kalu Ram was dressed and waiting for him. Ramu bent down and touched his father's feet.

'May you live to be a hundred years old, my son,' said Kalu Ram.

Having got his blessings, Ramu was all ready for the walk ahead. His heart felt light once more as he stepped onto the lane. Today he let Ajit and Chotu go on ahead, for sometimes he liked to walk alone.

Vidya Bhavan School was just about a mile from the city gates. It was outside the town and the air was fresh. There were no houses around the small grey building. A wire fence kept the cows from wandering into the large compound. As he walked, Ramu thought about the court-yard, which was his favourite place in the school. In the courtyard, there were two mango trees with low branches that bore fruit and several lime trees with small, sweet-smelling flowers. All around the school there were vast open spaces where water buffalo grazed. On two sides, the fields were green, with long wheat stalks swaying gently. Next to the sugar cane was the sweet corn, but it could not be seen above the tall sugar cane. And far off, the end of the flat, open ground touched the hills whose slopes rose into the Aravali Range.

Perhaps school isn't such a bad place, thought Ramu as he took a book of verse from his bag and read, moving his lips. He could walk slowly now, for he was nearly there.

Other boys were starting to come in from all sides.

Most of them walked, but a few lucky ones had bicycles.

'Come on, leave that book—you will get blind if you study so hard,' one boy said as he nudged Ramu. That was Golu, the son of a wealthy shop owner. He always made fun of the other boys and teased them about their torn shoes and shabby clothes.

Ramu just smiled and continued to read.

'Here, can't you see where you're going?' said Golu as he purposely bumped into him. 'I might remind you that this isn't your father's private property where you can stroll as you wish,' he added pompously and laughed as he pushed Ramu off the road.

Ramu threw his bag on the ground, marched up to Golu, and demanded, 'What did you say about my father? I dare you to say it again.'

Golu laughed in his face and replied in an even voice, 'What has happened to our gentle little Ramu today? It seems he has had pepperwater this morning.' With these words Golu and his friends burst into laughter.

Before anyone realized, Ramu had given Golu a hard thump on the back which made him straighten with surprise.

'You dare to hit me?' screamed Golu. 'You will re-gret this day all right.' Quickly he took hold of Ramu's neck and socked him on the nose. Ramu managed to dodge the next wild swing and threw one hard punch right to Golu's stomach. Golu reeled back, not so much from pain but from the shock of having missed his easy target.

The crowd of spectators was growing larger and soon had made a circle around the two boys. Ramu looked small next to the tall, heavy Golu.

'Come on, Ramu,' they shouted. 'Come on.'

This time Ramu and Golu were like two wrestlers with hands intertwined and legs firmly on the ground.

'Throw him down, Ramu,' shouted the crowd. 'Throw him to the ground.'

The two boys remained motionless, hands locked tight, until Ramu suddenly let go. This threw Golu off balance. With the skill of a wrestler, Ramu bent down and jerked Golu's right leg up, throwing him to the ground. The fight was over and Ramu was victorious.

The crowd rejoiced, laughing and throwing books into the air.

As the boys started moving on to assembly, Ramu hurriedly dusted his pants, straightened his hair, and wiped his nose. When he tucked in his shirt, he saw that it was torn—his brand new shirt that his mother had put out for him that morning. He clenched his teeth and swallowed to push back the tears. Only one escaped and rolled onto his cheek. Ramu quickly wiped it away against his bag as he ran to join the school line.

The assembly was full, with the boys standing according to their classes. The headmaster stood in front with the school register. The roll call was taken and then the headmaster gave a short talk on the importance of being honest. At the end of the talk the boys folded their hands

and sang the school prayer. The assembly was dismissed and the boys filed out in pairs.

'Lucky that the headmaster didn't see Golu's swollen face,' whispered Chotu.

Ajit waited until the teacher had gone ahead, then said, 'I am glad Golu got a good thrashing at last. In the beginning I was really afraid for Ramu.'

'I hope this puts an end to Golu's boasting,' said Chotu with a sneer. 'We all know his father is richer than ours, but why does he have to remind us all the time!'

Ajit and Chotu entered their class. As they sat down in front of their wooden desks, they heard excited voices all around them talking about the wrestling match. No one saw the teacher walk in.

'What is all this noise about? Don't you know it is time to be quiet?' said Jain Sahib, the teacher of history.

The boys sprang to attention and said, 'Good morning, sir.'

Jain Sahib was a tall, thin man known for his strictness. He was respected and feared by the boys. He folded his hands in response to their greeting, then said, 'Well, boys, today we will talk a little about the Mughal emperors. You know that the Udaipur Maharanas fought bravely against these emperors. Every child of India knows the great name of Maharana Pratap.' As he turned around to write the name of the king on the blackboard, Golu scribbled something on a piece of paper and was just about to pass it to his friend when the teacher caught him. 'What are you passing, Golu? Come here and show it to me,' said Jain Sahib in a severe tone.

'It is nothing, sir,' said Golu, quickly crumpling the paper.

'Golu, you are the last boy in the class who can afford to play. You have failed in all your weekly tests. I can't force you to work, but since you are not interested in your lessons, you can leave the class.'

Golu returned to his seat.

The students did not dare look at each other. They sat motionless and stared ahead, with eyes wide open.

'Now let us turn to page 42, on the great Mughal Emperor Akbar.'

Just then, the school orderly walked in with a notice. Jain Sahib read the note aloud. 'School will be closed one week for Diwali.'

Six days' holiday instead of the usual four was good news, but no one made a sound. The boys even seemed eager to continue with the great Emperor Akbar. They were not taking any chances with Jain Sahib.

'There is no point in starting a new chapter today. I will give you the homework I want done during the holidays and will take no excuses. There will be a test on the Monday that you return.' The master began writing on the blackboard, and the boys took out their notebooks and copied every word.

At last the period was over and the boys relaxed as Jain Sahib walked out of the class. The moment he was gone there was the opening and closing of desks and the chatter of the boys. They seemed relieved, stretching and yawning.

Now they cheerfully awaited the English lesson and their teacher, Mani Sahib. He was the favourite of the whole school. He had a small paunch, and winter and summer his bald head was covered with a knitted cap. The pockets of his shirt, which hung down over his dhoti, were always bulging. When he would walk into the classroom the boys would shout loudly, 'Good morning, sir!' Mani Sahib would step slowly on to the wooden platform and begin emptying his pockets until he found his large dark-rimmed glasses.

When Mani Sahib came into the classroom that Saturday, he said, 'I don't suppose you boys want to work today?'

'No, sir,' they all shouted together.

'Quiet! You will disturb the other classes. You are lucky to have two extra days. When I was a boy things were different.' His eyes took in the whole room, then he looked up and down the rows. When he spotted Ramu, he asked, 'Where were you yesterday?'

Golu saw his chance at last. 'Sir,' he said, jumping up, 'Ramu was at the mela yesterday. He didn't come to school.'

There was silence. Mani Sahib's gentle expression vanished. 'Come here, Golu. Come up here in front of the class.'

Mani Sahib stared at Golu and spoke in a slow, stern voice. 'I am ashamed of you. What would your father think if he knew you told on a fellow student?' He turned to the class. 'If I ever again hear any of my boys telling tales on a fellow student, I will use the ruler. You come to school not only to learn what is written in books but to build your character.'

Golu hung his head in shame.

Mani Sahib began the English lesson, but the students were grave and uneasy. They had never seen Mani Sahib this way before. They faltered and hesitated as they struggled through their hour of English.

Finally, the first stroke of the school gong sounded. The boys put their books into their schoolbags, careful not to forget anything. Slowly they filed out of class. For the moment the joy of Diwali was forgotten.

the cane fields

As soon as the boys were outside, their excitement returned. Those with bicycles raced for the stand and unfastened the locks. They piled on—some balancing on the handlebars, others pedalling, and still others perched on the rear wheel. There were boys rolling on the grass, somersaulting, and shouting cheers into the air, frightening the cows away.

Ramu was nearing the gate when Chotu and Ajit caught up with him.

'What's wrong with you today, Ramu?' they asked. 'Why are you in such a hurry to get home? You should feel proud that you knocked that fat Golu down.'

But Ramu felt depressed about it all. He did not like fights and seldom got into one.

'Come on, Ramu, now is not the time to be sad. We have a wonderful idea,' said Ajit. 'Let's go into the fields and break a few sugar canes.'

'I don't think I will come today,' said Ramu, as he reached the gate. 'Perhaps another time.'

'But it will be such fun! And we know you can handle the chowkidar who patrols the fields. Don't let us down. After all that trouble in class, it will be so nice to peacefully chew and enjoy the sweet, juicy sugar cane.'

Ramu joined his two friends. They all jumped over the barbed-wire fence like experts, avoiding the sharp edges, and reached the other side of the school grounds.

The sugar cane field ran parallel to the road, and for poachers it was the easiest way to enter unnoticed. The three boys crept into the field and were soon lost in a jungle of slender, delicate sugar cane.

'Ah-h-h,' whispered Ajit, 'we are lucky. This is not the thick, hard cane that is impossible to cut through with the teeth.'

'Come this way. Here is a good spot,' called Ramu. 'No one will see us. We will be well under cover.'

The three moved farther into the field until they were in the midst of a luscious patch of stalks.

'Sh-sh, sh-sh,' said Ajit suddenly. 'I can hear steps.' The boys remained motionless and listened. From somewhere in the field there came the sound of footfalls and the snapping of the sugar cane. Then it grew still.

'Don't move,' whispered Ramu, 'it is the chowkidar trying to catch us red-handed.'

After a few seconds, the sound of approaching steps grew louder as the cane rustled and cracked. The boys stood frozen. Then Ajit said softly, 'Let's go before we are caught. I am sure it is the chowkidar.'

The three moved stealthily through the thickets of sugar cane, their heads lowered. As the sound increased, they crouched lower and struggled through the muddy field

toward the road. Finally, scratched and bleeding and breathless, they halted. 'We haven't a chance,' gasped Ramu.

Surrounded by the thick growth, the three huddled together and awaited their fate. Suddenly the sugar cane parted, and before them stood Golu and his friend, Lakhu. One of Golu's eyes was black and puffy and his arms and legs were covered with bruises. The boys stared at each other, then broke into wild shrieks of laughter.

'What a fright you gave us!' cried Ajit in relief. 'We were sure it was the chowkidar.'

'What about us?' broke in Golu. 'Just as Lakhu and I were about to break a stalk, we heard footsteps. We also were sure it was the chowkidar. We decided to run for our lives, only Lakhu got his leg caught and fell.' Golu pointed to the blood streaming down Lakhu's leg. Then he looked at Ramu as he said, 'But I kept running. I didn't feel like getting another thrashing today.'

Ramu put his arm around Golu's shoulders and said, 'Come, boys, let us at least break one sugar cane.'

'No, I can't bear it any longer,' said Ajit. 'Let us go. I have had enough.'

'We have made so much noise that the chowkidar must know something is wrong,' agreed Chotu.

But Ramu was not listening. He leaped into the nearest patch and broke off a long, tender sugar cane. At that moment there came a booming voice. 'Beware! Who goes there?' The boys jumped the ditch and ran. The echo of the chowkidar's voice followed them far down the road.

When the sound of the chowkidar's voice had faded, Ramu put the cane on his knee and snapped it into five pieces. He gave the longest one to Golu as a gesture of friendship. 'Lucky for us it was you who caught us and not the chowkidar,' said Ramu as he tore off the hard skin of the sugar cane with his teeth.

The boys walked along in silence, chewing the sweet, white cane and spitting the crushed parts into the ditch. They were all too tired and too busy savouring the cane to bother with the traffic. Today they walked in the dusty ditches on the sides of the road and let the cars pass by freely. At the Hathi-pol, they parted company. 'Good-bye, Golu. I am sorry for what I did this morning. I lost my temper,' said Ramu as he held out his hand.

'No, no, it was my fault,' said Golu, 'but I have learned my lesson.' He shook Ramu's hand.

Ramu gave Golu a friendly punch, waved good-bye to the other three and entered the maze of lanes to the right of the Elephant Gate.

When he came home, Ramu found his mother sitting on the doorstep, combing, oiling, and plaiting Munni's hair and keeping an eye on the grain and dal she had spread out on the street to dry. Always the sun had to get the damp out of the yearly stock, which was bought in large quantities when the grain was cheap.

His mother had just finished one braid and was shoo-ing the birds away when Munni saw Ramu. 'There is bhaiya. He has come, he has come,' she cried as she ran toward him with one side of her hair flying in the air.

'Come back. Let me finish your hair. . . ' But Munni had already clasped Ramu tight in her small arms.

'Bhaiya, bhaiya, I found the sack with your presents. Truly, they are beautiful—especially the clay queen. Tell me what you did at the mela.'

This was the last thing Ramu wanted to be reminded of. 'Not now, little mouse. Here is something else I saved for you.' And Ramu gave his favourite sister a piece of his sugar cane.

The sun rays were losing their warmth, and this was the moment to take in the grain. Ramu helped his mother gather up the grain and dal and bring them to the storeroom where they were kept in huge clay urns. No matter how often Ramu read to his mother of the new methods used to keep away the insects, she did not have much faith in it.

She continued to air the grain and dal every month and dust them carefully, picking out the small stones—just as her mother and grandmother had done before her.

'Ma, what fun we will have. In just two days it will be Diwali,' said Ramu as he came in with the sack of dal hanging down his back and dumped it on the floor near the big urns. The storeroom was small, dark, and musty, but everything was well arranged. In one corner was the stone grinder used for making wheat flour, and next to it was the metal grinder for spices. 'I saw the mouth organ, ma,' added Ramu. 'It is still hanging on a peg in Tulsi's shop. I asked him how much it cost.'

Ramu turned to his mother, but she showed no interest. She placed the lid securely on the urn, and left the storeroom to begin peeling potatoes for the evening meal.

Ramu stayed behind. He took down the box in which he kept his odds and ends and found the strings he needed to fix the violin. As he sat on the floor and worked on the violin, the rats scurried about, nibbling what they wanted. But Ramu did not mind the rats, for they were accepted as part of the family. The storeroom was their favourite playground, and Ramu thought they might even enjoy listening to him practise the songs he would sing that evening.

preparation for Diwali

When Ramu awoke the following morning, he could feel the excitement of Diwali. There were so many things to do to prepare for the visit of the Goddess Lakshmi. Each of the four small rooms in Ramu's house would be swept clean, and a fresh coating of cow dung would be spread over the floors and the courtyard. Everything had to look new and spotless.

While his mother was getting the vegetables from the woman next to the cow shed, Ramu got busy. He rolled up the straw mats and bedding and put them away on the shelves. He dusted the table and straightened the charpai, the one bed reserved for his father or for special guests.

He went out to the cow shed and fed the cow and her calf. As they ate, he leaned against them, scratching their foreheads and telling them about Diwali. The cows listened, lazily brushing away the flies with their tails. With a final pat, Ramu said, 'I am sorry, my friends, but today I cannot play. I must get ready for the Goddess Lakshmi.'

Ramu gathered up the cow dung and piled it in a corner. Later, his mother would make cow-dung cakes,

dry them in the sun, and use them for the fire instead of
wood.

Having changed the water in the trough and cleaned
out the shed, Ramu called Munni to help him, for she was
an expert at sweeping. He found her playing in front of
the house.

'Come on, Munni, get along with the sweeping.
Otherwise, we will be late.' Munni quickly took hold of
the hand broom, got on to her haunches, and began to push
the rubbish along with the mud. Her hands went swiftly
over the ground and she moved on her haunches like a frog.

'Ramu,' called his mother from inside the house.

Ramu washed his hands, dried them on the sides of his pants and went in.

'Beta,' said his mother as she laid down the vegetables near the fireplace, 'I forgot to get extra oil and ghee fc Diwali, and from tomorrow the shops will be closed Run quickly and get some for me.'

'Yes, ma. And what about the earthen saucers'. Have we enough to light the whole house?'

'I have fifty from last year and I will buy another fifty from the man who comes with his donkey. He sells them cheaper than you will find in the market.'

'Then, ma, I will also get the firecrackers and the sweets.'

'No, no. The sweets your father will get. You go now and get the oil, and maybe a few firecrackers. Don't get the expensive ones, and go to the grocer next to Ratu's pan shop.' She gave Ramu some money for the oil and two rupees for the firecrackers.

'Ma, can't I have a little more money for the sparklers? And I will have some other special shopping to do, too. It is Diwali,' said Ramu as he looked at the rupees in his hand.

'Beta, this year we will have to make do with what we have. Now run along and stop grumbling.'

Hearing the conversation, Munni threw down her broom and ran into the kitchen. 'Bhaiya, I am coming, too.' She put her hand out and asked, 'Ma, give me some money. I will also buy something.'

'No, Ramu cannot take you with him. It is not proper for a girl to be seen in the city bazaar.'

Munni let out a wail and sat down rubbing her eyes.

'Come, help me with the cooking,' said her mother, 'and leave Ramu to do the shopping.'

Ramu promised to buy his sister a special present with the secret money he had saved and hurried to the bazaar. It lay around the Clock Tower in the centre of the old city, and everyone flocked there to hear the gossip and do their shopping. Today it was in a state of excitement. Workers were standing on the parapet of the great Jagdish Temple with its one thousand steps, giving it a good cleaning. Shopkeepers were rearranging their goods, taking out the best for display and polishing them to make them look new. Shops selling pots and pans were doing quick business, for everyone got a new metal vessel for Diwali. The rich bought vessels made of silver, while the villagers thronged the brassware shops. Bright saris of red and green and every colour hung from shop ceilings and fluttered in the air.

All the shops were decorated, some with paper frills and others with fresh flowers. Even the small vendors had put coloured paper around their carts and stuck balloons in the midst of their peanuts and hot gram. Religious music filled the air, and everywhere there was the scent of the sandalwood incense sticks that burned before the image of the Goddess Lakshmi.

Threading his way through the crowds, Ramu came to the place of Ratu, the pan-wala. Inside his cabin on a raised wooden seat surrounded by all makes of cigarettes and piles of cheap tobaccos, he sat grinning. His teeth and fingers were stained a dark red from chewing the tasty green leaf. Ramu had many times watched Ratu spread the pan leaf thick with the lime and katha paste. Today Ratu was busy serving his customers.

Next to Ratu's shop was the grocery store. As Ramu passed through the doorway strung with beads, the din outside faded. The sound of the religious songs now grew distant.

Inside the store heaps of earthen saucers and firecrackers were piled on the floor, and in a far corner was a huge bundle of fluffed cotton used for making wicks for the Diwali lamps.

Ramu bought the ghee and oil and hung the bottles by a string over his shoulder. Then he turned back to the grocer.

'Dada,' he asked, 'how much are the firecrackers?'

'I have a hundred different kinds,' said the man. 'These rockets that burst into the air like a million stars sell for one rupee each. But these big pomegranates are eight annas, and the smaller ones go for only four annas apiece.'

Ramu felt in his pocket for the two rupees his mother had given him. 'That is still too much for me,' he said. 'Have you nothing cheaper?'

'For only four annas I can give you a box of twelve sparklers,' said the grocer. 'Then there are the small bombs. You light the wick and run away—and *bang*, off it goes with a loud crash! And there's something new this year—the snake. You light its tail and it wriggles and hisses. Then it bursts into coloured sparks. They are great fun—my children love them. And they are only two annas each.'

Ramu tried to make a selection, but soon gave up.

'Dada, here is one rupee. Give me what you think is best—but not too many sparklers, please.'

The grocer unfastened several bundles, counted out the firecrackers, and rolled Ramu's order up in a large sheet of newspaper. Then he took an extra pomegranate and held it out to Ramu.

'Beta, this is your present for Diwali.'

Ramu thanked the grocer and tucked the bundle under his arm. As he turned toward home, he heard the pan-wala call out. 'Ramu, what's your hurry today? At least come and take your pan.'

Ramu went eagerly and squatted in front of Ratu's little shop.

'Ratu, dada, are you going to see the illuminations at the main palace this year? The Lake Palaces are also going to be lit.'

'Can anyone miss seeing the palaces at Diwali? Even the elephants will march in procession all decorated with silver ornaments as in the old days.'

Ramu's eyes opened wide as thoughts of his dream returned. He remembered the great painted beasts lumbering down the road, and the Maharana holding out his glittering hand. Could it be, he asked himself, that his dream could come to life?

'Ramu,' came his father's voice, 'what are you doing here on a Sunday morning?'

Ramu started and looked into the face of Kalu Ram.

'You should be home cleaning the cow shed,' continued his father.

Ramu finally found his tongue. 'Ma sent me to buy oil,' he answered respectfully.

'Well, you must go home now. There is still much to be done before the Goddess Lakshmi visits us.'

'But, dada, there is the special shopping I must do. I have told ma already,' said Ramu.

Kalu Ram presented Ratu with a package of sweets. 'May you have a joyous Diwali.'

Ratu received the large bundle with both hands and raised it to his forehead in a gesture of gratitude. 'And for you, Kalu Ram and Ramu, I have specially prepared two of my finest pans.'

Kalu Ram and his son bowed to the pan-wala and joined the crowds that swarmed outside the busy silver-smiths. Everywhere there were men shopping for their womenfolk—trying to see whether the silver bracelets and anklets were the right size, and then weighing them to determine the price.

'Dada.' Ramu stopped his father by the last shop. 'Don't you want to look, also?'

'No, Ramu. It is our shop I want you to see first. It shines with much cleaning and fine paper decorations. Truly, it is beautiful.'

On their way out of the main street, they met the man who went from door to door with his donkey, selling the tiny earthen saucers. Now his basket was empty and he was heading home, glad to be through with his business so early in the day. With a wide grin, he wished Kalu Ram and Ramu a prosperous Diwali.

Kalu Ram's shop was small and modest. It stood on the street of sweet shops that led off from the centre of the main bazaar. Here, too, there was a rush of activity, for Diwali was a time of making special sweets of all shapes and colours.

When they reached his father's shop, Ramu's uncle was packing curled wafers soaked in syrup into earthen cups. He always helped out when business was heavy, and today he did not even have time to say hello.

Kalu Ram's shop did not have the modern glass jars or the brass vases with sweet-smelling flowers or pictures on the wall, but it was clean and tidy. A cloth embroidered with big sunflowers and daisies was heaped high with yellow and orange candy balls. From the ceiling hung a thin line of intertwined leaves, and incense sticks burned in the corner.

'Dada, it is very nice,' said Ramu. But his eyes were drawn to Hari's sweet shop across the way. It was indeed a magnificent place, with many helpers. Some were kneading flour; others were rolling out the dough; and a man sat frying corn flour wafers. Hari also had the gadgets and moulds to make sweets in the shape of birds and beasts and even figures of children. As Ramu looked over at the fancy wrapping paper and tinsel, Hari saw him and smiled. 'Ramu! What a privilege to have you with us.' He selected a small basket filled with toy sweets and brought it over.

Ramu thanked Hari and hungrily took the Diwali present. In seconds he had nibbled the beaks and legs from the sweets, but he remembered to save some for his sisters.

'We will visit the churi-wali next,' said Kalu Ram, as he and Ramu left their shop. Back on the busy main road, they took a turn onto a quieter side street and came to the churi-wali sitting in the sun. At her side was a large basket filled with bangles of coloured glass, and spread on a cloth before her were bead necklaces of golds and silvers, reds and greens.

'Babuji, something for Diwali?' she asked, looking up at Kalu Ram.

'Bibi, I will have six silver bangles for a child of seven.'

The churi-wali hurriedly opened a box and showed Kalu Ram a fine selection.

'They are very handsome. I will take these and another six for someone with hands like yours.'

The woman smiled, for she understood for whom they

were meant. She opened a new box and took out six lovely red and green glass bangles, tried them on, then held them before Kalu Ram. He nodded approval, paid the churi-wali for the order, and wished her happiness for Diwali.

As father and son entered another gulli, a boy who sat in a drab wooden shop asked, 'Don't you want to buy something from me, Babuji? No one buys from me because my shop is not in the bazaar. But my things are just as good and much cheaper.'

'Where is your father today?' asked Kalu Ram.

'He has been sick with a fever for ten days, and no one knows what it is.'

'I am sorry to hear this.' Kalu Ram looked around the little shop, which seemed rather sad. 'What toys do you have?' he asked. 'I need something for my small daughter.'

'Sir, I have toys of all kinds,' said the boy. 'But I know what a little girl of four will like. See, here is a cooking set.' The boy jumped up and took down a basket. Inside was a rolling pin for rotis, two buckets, a frying pan and a small stove. All were a bright red and green colour.

Kalu Ram bought the cooking set for Ganga and also a wooden bat and ball with which she could play in the courtyard.

As they were leaving, Ramu fingered the coins in his pocket. 'Father,' he said, 'I have six annas. Could we go to Bor Wadi for a few minutes? I am sure to find something there for ma and Munni and Ganga. In the big bazaar nothing is cheap; everything costs too much.'

Kalu Ram pondered a while. 'Ramu, while you go to Bor Wadi, I will have my beard shaved. I haven't had a real shave for a week.'

Ramu left his father and walked towards the Bor Wadi stalls where all kinds of fruits, sugar cane, and nuts lay in cone-shaped heaps that tempted children and hungry flies.

The flies are having their day, too, thought Ramu as he saw a whole army of them spread over a heap of sticky dates. Even when he passed, they did not move.

Ramu darted towards the alley by the Clock Tower which stood at the head of Bor Wadi. Suddenly, along the road came a tonga at full speed. Ramu jumped aside just in time.

'Look where you are going,' called the driver, merrily waving his switch as the horse-buggy rattled by.

The Bor Wadi lane was dark and so narrow that only two people could pass through at a time. Here the villagers and poor people of the city came to shop. Along the muddy lane men sat on their platforms made of packing cases and huddled amid their goods with hardly any room to move. Even the ceilings of the shops were so low that one had to crouch beneath them.

Ramu headed straight for Tulsi's wooden cabin. There he found his old friend with the long, white beard half dozing, a fly sitting on his nose. Softly, Ramu tiptoed in among stacks of boxes, and eased himself through a

thick curtain of tassels and bells that hung down from the low beams. A few more steps and he saw his mouth organ swaying in the corner. Ramu reached out his hand and gently touched it, murmuring, 'We have waited for each other such a long time, my friend. It would not be right for you to belong to anyone else.'

As Ramu stepped back into the sunlight, Tulsi stirred.

'Ah, Ramu, I thought you would come today. Perhaps for Diwali the mouth organ will be yours.'

'I wish for nothing else,' sighed Ramu.

He moved quickly by the next few stalls, then crossed to the other side of the gulli and went straight to the little shop where he knew he could find presents for his sisters.

'Have you anything for the hair?' Ramu asked the shopkeeper who wore a pair of striped pyjamas stretched tightly across his bulging stomach.

'What I have you won't ever find in the big bazaar,' said the churi-wala. 'Look here—have you seen this before?'

He opened a long cardboard box. Inside were coloured butterfly hair clips made of new plastic material. Another box that the shopkeeper brought out was filled with coloured glass dots that the Hindu women stick in the middle of their foreheads.

Ramu was so excited that, even before he knew how much they cost, he ordered two butterfly hair clips and eight glass dots. How happy Munni and Ganga would be—and his mother could not find anything more lovely than those fancy dots! Ramu paid the man and thanked him.

With his remaining two annas, he hurried to the tobacco shop at the end of the lane. Freshly-baked clay pipes lay in a great mass, and Ramu smiled as he thought of how much his father enjoyed smoking a pipe after dinner. Carefully he chose two pipes and paid one anna.

'What about a little tobacco, boy!' asked the man.

'I have only one anna left,' said Ramu. 'Will that be enough?'

The man nodded cheerfully and wrapped some strong black tobacco in a piece of newspaper.

Ramu was very pleased as he walked back to the Clock Tower. His father stood waiting for him, his face freshly shaven and his hands full of gifts.

'What have you got there?' asked Kalu Ram, eyeing Ramu's packages.

'I knew I would find all I wanted in Bor Wadi, father.' Ramu got into stride with Kalu Ram and soon they were back in the familiar old gulli.

'Ah-h-h,' breathed Ramu and his father as they approached their home. How handsome it had become! Ramu's mother had already painted the Om sign on the walls and put a wreath of banana leaves around the frame of the door to welcome the gods and goddesses.

While Kalu Ram and Ramu were taking off their shoes on the doorstep, Munni flung open the door.

'Bapuji, bapuji, what have you got in the parcels?' she cried, clapping her hands. Little Ganga was close behind.

Kalu Ram swept Ganga into his arms, gave Munni a wink, and led the procession into the kitchen.

Everything glowed with beauty, and delicious food smells filled the room. In the middle of the floor, Ramu's mother was putting the last touches to the yellow circle of powdered rice with the Om symbol in the centre. She wore an emerald-green sari over a choli and skirt. As she worked, the bangles on her wrists and ankles jingled. Always on festival days she covered herself with all her jewellery. How gay it made her feel, and how cheerful it made the whole house!

Ramu put the bottles of oil on the shelf, then he began to open the package of firecrackers.

'Not now, beta,' his mother called. 'Go and wash your hands and feet and get ready to eat.'

The mats were spread, and two metal thallis were placed on them. Four small cups with vegetables and dal were placed upon the thallis.

Ramu and his father ate together from the big thalli, while Munni and Ganga ate from the smaller one. Ramu's mother sat near the fire, rolling the dough for purees. As each puree puffed up in the pan, she removed it and put a new one into the sizzling oil. Ramu and his father devoured them faster than they could be rolled. The little girls had fun just pricking the puffed purees and watching them collapse.

Next, Ramu's mother served the halwa.

After their meal, Munni and Ganga were each allowed to open one present. Ganga loved the cooking set. But when Munni saw the butterfly hair clip Ramu had bought her, she ran out into the street to show it to her friends.

Ramu watched his mother open the small package of coloured glass dots. Tears came to her eyes. She looked

at her son, unable to speak, and drew him close to her.
'May God protect you, beta. And may you live to be a
hundred years.'

Now it was Kalu Ram's turn. He was so touched by
the clay pipes and the scented tobacco that he found it hard
to control his tears. He looked over at Ramu's mother and
a quiet sadness filled the room. At last, Kalu Ram spoke.
His voice was heavy.

'Ramu, it saddens me that I must speak to you like
this, but you have to learn that in life you must work hard
and honestly if you are to receive the blessing of the
Goddess of Knowledge. Last Friday you missed school,
and I must punish you for it, beta. But it is for your own
good. The mouth organ that you have wanted for so long
will not be yours for Diwali.'

Ramu bowed his head and cast his eyes on the floor.
His heart felt empty. He wanted to be alone.

the picnic

All night Ramu slept soundly. Not even the rats that scampered over him and gnawed the sacks of puffed rice disturbed him.

At dawn he got up. Somewhere inside of him he still felt a stab of sadness. But as he mashed the fodder, oil, and wheat husks for the cows in a large pail of fresh water, the dull ache vanished.

In the shed, the cow and her calf gave him a sleepy greeting and munched their breakfast while he told them about the picnic Golu's father had planned and that he would not be back until evening.

After he milked the cow and brought the pitcher back into the kitchen, he took one of the large earthenware pots and left for the public water tap. It was not far from his house and at this early hour there would not be a crowd waiting in line.

He reached the tap where there were only two women ahead of him. When they had gone, Ramu gathered his dhoti around him and had a bath. Then he filled his pitcher with water and carried it back to his house.

Ramu's mother was in the kitchen, collecting the pots and pans she was taking to the picnic. Golu's mother was supplying the food.

'What a good, helpful boy you are,' Ramu's mother said as she took the splashing pitcher from him. 'Now, beta, please get the two papayas I put in the storeroom to ripen—and also the packet of salted wafers. It will be nice to bring something special to the picnic.'

Kalu Ram took his bath, and the girls had their hair braided and the soothing black kohl was placed on the inner rims of their eyes. Then they all sat down to a light breakfast. Not long after they had finished, the horse's hooves sounded in the gulli, and the tonga came to a stop in front of their house.

In the back seat of the tonga sat Golu's mother and sister. Munni and Ganga squeezed in next to them, leaving room for their mother. The provisions and gunny sack were put at the driver's feet. The place next to him was reserved for Chotu's mother.

Kalu Ram locked the house, and he and Ramu walked to the temple. There they met Ajit, Chotu, and Golu who were with their fathers. The men decided to follow the tonga route to the picnic, but Ramu and his friends had another idea.

'Father,' asked Ramu, who was voted the leader, 'may we boys take the short cut along the side of Machla Mungra Hill? We can then help to make the fire.'

'I know, you boys want to see the zoo,' said Kalu Ram, with a wink. 'Run along then!'

The men waved good-bye, leaving the boys happily nudging each other.

'To the mango grove and the Gulab Bagh,' shouted Ramu. And together the four set out at a run, throwing their heads back to catch the cool air. Through the western Gate of the Sun and across the side of the hill they raced. The day was perfect and the sun's rays were soft and soothing. Many families were going on outings. Some were riding in tongas and rickshas, but most of them were walking. Mithoo, the ricksha-wala, passed by, breathlessly pumping the pedals of his ricksha. When he saw Ramu, he called out, 'And where are you off to today?'

'To Machla Mungra,' answered the boys.

But Ramu got a strange feeling. The sight of Mithoo and his ricksha recalled to him the day he had stolen away to the mela. Again for a moment he thought of his mouth organ, the Diwali gift he had lost.

Ahead of the boys lay the Gulab Bagh, an immense public park which was once the property of the maharanas of Udaipur. Trees laden with many fruits grew here—mangos and plums, limes, oranges and guavas. And every-where there was the smell of the wild jasmine flower.

The boys' eyes set on the ripe guavas. Then Ajit caught Ramu's gaze and asked slyly, 'What are you think-ing about, Ramu?'

Ramu stole his eyes away from the guava grove. 'I was just wondering if the old lion is still alive,' he said hurriedly.

'Are you joking!' Ajit laughed.

The other boys understood. 'Let's try to do better

this time,' said Chotu, impatient to begin, 'and not be as stupid as we were on Saturday. Only two of us must enter the grove. The other two will keep watch.'

'That's a wonderful plan,' Golu said, hoping he would be chosen to watch.

He put his hands to his face and felt the sore spots. He was in no mood to be scratched again. Luckily for him, Ramu and Ajit decided to go.

The four boys moved silently along the edge of the lawn, keeping off the forbidden grass. They stopped before the marble statue of the brave Alsatian dog who died saving a maharana from a tiger.

When they reached the guava grove at the far end of the park, Ramu and Ajit entered the cluster of small trees. For the two boys who nervously watched and waited, it seemed ages before Ramu came out, his trouser pockets bulging.

'Where is Ajit?' breathed Golu. 'Let us be on our way.'

As they waited for Ajit to appear, a man came towards them. They paid no attention since he looked like any other stroller.

'How do you like the guavas?' asked the man as he came up to them. 'Look at the poor branches drooping heavily. Pick the ripe guavas—go on! It is Diwali, and you know how our Maharana loves children.'

The boys stood frozen.

'Imagine that,' said the man, shaking his head, 'the

chief chowkidar gives you permission to pick the fruits, and still you hesitate! What amazing boys,' he mumbled and continued on his inspection round.

When Ajit crept out, his hands full of the sweet red guavas, the boys looked at each other in shame.

'Look what I have!' announced Ajit.

When his friends showed no eagerness, he asked, 'What's wrong? Have you just seen the ghost of the chowkidar?'

'No,' said Golu, still trembling, 'only the chief chowkidar himself.'

Slightly dazed, they hurried on. They passed the zoo where a great lion sunned himself, and his lioness padded majestically around in their cage. But the boys did not stop to say hello to the king of the forest.

After clearing the west boundary of the park, they hopped across a stream and began a breathless rush up the hill.

Halfway to the top, they spotted the women busily unpacking the picnic supplies. They had chosen a shady place on a stretch of level ground which faced the vast blue lakes below.

'Ramu! Where have you been?' shouted his mother as she saw him. 'And where are the menfolk? What will they say when they find we have not started the fire?'

Without a word, the boys scattered into the forest, collecting wood and dry twigs. Within minutes they were back, their arms piled high.

Ramu placed three large stones together in a semi-circle, forming the fireplace. Inside the circle he put dried leaves and twigs, laid the thicker branches on top, and watched the fire come to life.

The women had already peeled and cut the potatoes which were soaking in the gram-flour batter. Munni and Golu's sister were shelling the new green peas, chattering and giggling as they worked. Ganga roamed about, eating the pea seeds from the empty pods. Golu's mother had stuffed the tender purple and green brinjals with a tasty mixture and had chopped the onions and tomatoes together.

Soon the men arrived, panting and mopping their brows. They sat down to rest, and the boys joined them. The women spread banana leaves in front of the men and, at a little distance away, set a group of mats for themselves. From the smouldering coals and hot ash came the smell of roasting sweet corn.

First Munni and her friend served the chopped onions. Then the women brought the flat green leaves laden with vegetables and the corn bread dripping with butter. The boys needed no coaxing. The corn bread and vegetables seemed much tastier than when they ate them on the floor in their homes.

When the men had finished lunch, Golu collected the banana leaves and piled them in the forest away from the stray dogs that had already gathered nearby. Except for an occasional yelp from the dogs as they rooted through

the garbage, a contented quiet came over the group. The
good lunch made the men drowsy. Even the betel nuts
and candy tidbits did not tempt them. Now it was the
women's turn to eat. They sat down with their backs to
the men and began their lunch.

Ramu and his friends tucked the tasty pan leaves into
their pockets and slipped away to explore.

'Boys,' called Golu's father after them, 'the forests
are not safe after sundown. Be sure to be back before
dark.'

Once on their own, the four boys headed straight for the forests that encircled Machla Mungra. It was in a fortress on the hill that the maharanas of Udaipur kept the arsenal of guns and powder to protect the ancient city from invading armies.

Thump. Thump. Two stones whizzed past Golu's head.

'Help! I am being attacked,' he cried, and crouched low to the ground.

'What's the matter with you?' asked Ramu. 'The monkeys probably think you're a tiger. Stand up and be brave.'

'But . . .' Before he could say more, a hail of pebbles flew at them, some missing by inches.

'Ho,' shouted Chotu, as they ducked. 'A mad hunter is loose up there. We must get to the clearing before one of those stones breaks our heads open.'

As they banded together and headed for the clearing, Ramu saw they were only three. 'Where is Ajit?' he asked. The boys looked about them but he was nowhere in sight.

'Aha,' said Ramu. 'That Ajit is up to mischief.'

Cautiously, the three crawled out into the meadow. There, in the thick of the jungle, was one of the royal shooting boxes. And sitting inside the box with his slingshot was Ajit.

The boys moved around to the back of the hideout to take Ajit by surprise.

'Ho,' called Ramu. 'Here is our mad hunter.'

'What did you think of my aim?' Ajit asked as he saw Golu's white face.

'I thought I was dead,' said Golu.

The four burst into laughter and, grabbing hands, raced wildly over the meadow and into the forest.

The farther into the forest they went, the thicker and darker it became. But the boys felt safe. Ramu carried a strong stick, and Ajit had his sling and a pocketful of pebbles. They were in such good spirits that it was a long time before the deep silence of the forest made them uncomfortable. The only sounds came from the plaintive cooing of the birds and the rustling of the leaves as huge, black-faced monkeys jumped from branch to branch.

'Look! There goes a rabbit,' said Ramu.

'And there's another,' said Ajit. 'They probably heard our footsteps and thought we were hunters.'

'Sh . . . sh, sh . . . sh,' whispered Golu. 'What is that noise?'

'Over here,' called Chotu. 'Look! Look quick! Two peacocks are dancing in the sunshine.'

Ahead in the path, two peacocks, their fans fully spread, pranced together in a shaft of light. Sun specks caught in their rich, golden-blue feathers and glistened as the plumes swayed back and forth. The sight became more dazzling as a horde of peacocks joined the pair in a stately procession down the path.

'We cannot waste time if we are to reach the village

and see the pit where the tigers fought the wild boars,' said Chotu, going on alone.

Ramu, who was dawdling and taking his time, noticed the pug marks of an animal and bent down for a closer look. 'Boys, come and see—I am sure these are the signs of a panther.'

Ajit, Golu, and Chotu came and squatted on their haunches as they carefully examined the marks in the wet ground.

'These are the prints of a panther, all right,' said Ajit. 'He probably came down from the forest to drink at the lakes.'

'We must hurry,' pleaded Golu.

The group left the dense forest. After walking a short distance, they saw the huge, grey-black pit which was the landmark of the village.

'Last one there will be fed to a panther,' said Ramu, bursting into a sprint.

All four nearly collapsed as they reached the edge of the pit. Before they had regained their breath, a group of village boys surrounded them.

'Where are you from?' they asked.

'From the city.' Ramu spoke in English.

The village boys just stared back. Then an older boy asked, 'What language is that?'

'It is English,' answered Ramu proudly. 'We go to school where we learn to read and write in English.'

'It is very difficult,' added Ajit.

The village boys were impressed and led the visitors into the arena that surrounded the pit as though they were kings come to see a fight between a tiger and a wild boar. Inside, the rows of seats slanted up from the pit. They were cracked and broken and grass grew between the cement blocks. But, once, hundreds of people had crowded into this arena.

'Here is the gate for the tiger,' said a village boy. 'And over here the gate for the wild boar.'

The sight of the heavy iron gates that years ago had closed—trapping the animals—made the boys shiver.

Ramu and his friends sat down on the steps with the village boys and stretched out their legs. They reached into their pockets for the sweets they had saved, and passed around the nut-flavoured pan.

'What are those other villagers doing under the banyan tree?' asked Chotu.

'They are watching a cock fight,' answered one of the boys. 'It will soon be over.'

'Isn't it time we headed home?' said Golu. 'I, for one, don't want to go through the forest at night.'

Ramu and the others looked up at the sky. The sun was falling fast and the shadows had grown longer and blacker.

'There is a way that avoids the forest,' said one of the older village boys. 'We will take you to it.'

The group dipped down a slope, walked through a section of woods, and came out on to a narrow, well-worn path.

'Now don't leave this path,' the boy said. 'Keep straight on it and you will come to Lake Pichola. It is the longer way, but safe.'

The four boys were grateful to know the way. They said good-bye to the kind villagers and, moving single file, started home.

They walked fast and no one spoke. The winter darkness closed in around them and already the wild dogs had begun to howl. A surprised mongoose flashed between their legs and the cries of hyenas could be heard from afar. Ajit loaded his sling in case it was needed, and Golu took giant strides and was way ahead of the others.

At last the lake waters came into sight and they saw their fathers pacing up and down the embankment, awaiting their return.

'You boys certainly gave us a fright,' said Golu's father. 'Just last week a boy was bitten by a snake. Come on now, the tonga with the women and children has left long ago.'

Ramu sat down on the embankment and removed a thorn from his foot. The others lifted their dhotis and soaked their feet. They threw a little water over their faces, and were ready.

Even though their feet were sore, the boys didn't care. It had been a wonderful day. And as they walked along, they broke into song, loud and off-key. None of them was much of a singer.

Diwali festival of lights

On the day of Diwali, Ramu was up with only the stars and the cries of the jackals to keep him company. He bathed, then later he helped his mother with the final preparations for the Goddess Lakshmi's visit. His home would not disappoint her. It glowed with beauty.

In the courtyard, the cow and her calf, dressed in their finery, also waited to greet the Goddess. Across their backs lay the patchwork coats of red, green, and white. Their foreheads were marked with the red kum-kum powder, and a black line of kohl circled each eye. Their bright yellow hooves shone in the sun, and the bells on their necks tinkled as they moved. Ramu felt a surge of love for his cows. Such a sight, he thought, would surely bring a special smile to Lakshmi's face. And he knew well that a blessing from the Goddess could give a poor family a new life of comfort and wealth. This thought carried Ramu in a daze through the kitchen and out into the gulli to admire the front of his house. The morning had passed rapidly and it was close to noon. Sunlight glinted off the earthen saucers that lined the tiled roof and brightened the colours of the painted symbols.

As he stood in the gulli, Ramu heard laughter and singing. A band of children rounded the corner and raced up the steps of the rich haveli next door. Every child was welcome in every home. And the children would leave the haveli with their pockets filled with sweets.

'Ramu!' came a familiar shout. Ramu turned just as Ajit and Chotu reached his doorstep.

'What are you doing here?' panted Chotu. 'Don't you know this is Diwali? The elephants have already left the palace. We will never see them unless you hurry.'

'Come on!' urged Ajit.

And the three barefooted boys set off at a gallop toward Hathi-pol.

They were soon forced to walk. From every doorway in the city people poured forth into the lanes that led to the main road. Slowly the boys pushed their way through the throngs, trying their best to stay together. All along the route, from the Gate of Elephants to the great Jagdish Temple, people gathered on walls and roofs, peered out of windows, and climbed trees and poles to get a view of the royal procession. Children ran screaming, looking for last-minute places from which they could watch.

Then, above the great noise of the crowd, came the call of the flutes; and the ground trembled under the footfalls of the mighty elephants. A hush fell upon the crowd as the lead elephant, carrying the Maharana, came into view. So huge was the royal beast that he seemed to block out the sun. Rich brocades and silks hung from his painted body, and the golden jewels around his ankles and neck rattled with each step.

Behind the great beast's head perched the mahout dressed in a fitted silk coat with an orange turban. Gently he guided his elephant with a trident-shaped gaff. Sitting in a golden saddle on the peak of the elephant's back was the Maharana. On his head he wore a turban with the royal crest, and chains of diamonds, emeralds, and pearls flowed down the front of his court dress. His attendants walked alongside the elephant, holding their long peacock fans.

Next in line came two elephants draped in silver, carrying the princes with their plumes fluttering in the breeze. At the rear of the procession were eight baby elephants, with the flute players, drummers, and courtiers.

Only in his dream had Ramu seen such splendour. Yet here was his dream close enough to touch. Maybe if he shut his eyes, his mouth organ would return—and this time he would catch it.

Showers of rose petals fell from windows and rooftops. The crowd broke into song, clapping and cheering for their Maharana. When the Maharana raised his hand to accept their greeting, the royal elephant lifted his trunk and curled it back. The crowd cheered louder.

As the procession neared the Jagdish Temple, the flute players began the hymn of praise to the Goddess Lakshmi, the temple drums sounded, and six priests filed down the steps chanting the hymn. In their hands they carried lamps of burning incense, two sacred conch shells, and huge silver platters piled high with the blessed sweets.

At the foot of the steps the elephants stood motionless, facing the priests. Suddenly Ramu felt himself being swept by a river of people into the square.

The priests were reciting the holy verses. When they finished, temple bells pealed triumphantly, elephants lifted garlands of marigold in offering to the Goddess Lakshmi,

then gathered the rose petals in their trunks and scattered them upon the steps of the temple. Children squealed and wriggled with excitement as they gave sugar balls to the baby elephants and watched the head temple priest feed the royal elephant. Then the conch shells blew, the elephants raised their trunks in a final salute, swung around, and headed back to Fateh Sagar Lake and the palace.

Gradually the crowds drifted away from the square. Ramu looked about for Ajit and Chotu. They must have followed the procession out of the city, for he was all alone. In the street and on the temple steps lay thousands and thousands of garlands. They belonged to no one. Ramu picked one up, then another and another. He chose only the perfect ones to take to his mother.

The flaming orange of the sun faded below the city walls, leaving the sky a dusky blue. Ramu had gathered all the flowers he could hold, and he stood in front of the great temple doors before going inside. He knew he would be coming with his family for the last worship later that night, but there were things he wished to tell the Goddess in private.

At first he could not find the divine Goddess. Rows and rows of people—some standing with folded hands, others kneeling—packed every inch of space. But then he saw her, and her radiance was so sharp he had to blink back the tears. From her tiny ears dangled earrings of precious stones, and strings of pearls fell from either side of her forehead. On her festive clothes were pins made

of rubies, emeralds, and diamonds. Her wrists and ankles
sparkled with bracelets of gold and rare stones, and a chain
of pure gold surrounded her waist. Before her lay large
silver plates laden with sweets, and a sea of flowers covered
the ground. Men, women, and children were throwing
coins at her feet.

Slowly Ramu went to her and, kneeling down, touched
his forehead to the ground before her. Then he sat cross-
legged and looked into her kind eyes and felt her power.

'Mother of us All,' he prayed, 'you have brought my

dream to life. I did not earn such an honour. Dear Mother, help me to be a good boy. Make me worthy of all the things my family has done for me. And bless them.'

For a long moment Ramu sat amid the coins and flowers that covered the ground by Lakshmi's image and let his eyes travel over the high-domed room. Along the walls were large mirrors inlaid with gold that captured the flickering light from the wicks and reflected it into the warm dimness. Priests passed among the worshipers, murmuring prayers and handing out the sacred sweets and flowers. A group of men sat outside on the marble court-yard, singing the Ramayana and exalting the Lord's name.

Ramu wondered what it would be like to be a priest and live in this peaceful place. Then he rose, took a leaf-cup of sweets and quietly left. On either side of the broad stone steps crouched the beggars. Tonight they sat in silence, for the sound of the coins dropping into their bowls was like raindrops falling on a parched earth, and the blaze of the ten thousand lights from the temple gave them hope.

Ramu hurried through the narrow gullis. Coloured lights blazed in every shop, and from every house the wicks of a million earthen saucers sprang to life.

His father was waiting on the doorstep of his house. 'Ramu, beta,' he called, 'here are the matches. Climb quickly to the roof and light up our house. Ajit and Chotu are waiting for you there with the fireworks.'

From his rooftop, Ramu and his friends looked out over the city. Everywhere, millions and millions of lamps burned and flames danced in the air. It was as though a magic wand had touched the city of Udaipur.

In the lanes children set off bombs. Little girls put their hands to their ears as rockets shot into the air and burst, filling the sky with coloured stars.

Ramu, Ajit, and Chotu piled their fireworks together and started three sparklers at once. *Hiss-s-s-s!* The wild splash of sparks blurred their eyes and they laughed as the sticks burned down. Bombs, snakes, and a rocket went off in a twinkling. Only the empty shells remained, and Ramu's special pomegranate.

'Come, Ramu,' said Ajit and Chotu, 'yours is the last. Let us make a wish as we light it.' For a moment each stared into the night thinking his own secret.

With their supply gone, Ajit and Chotu had plans to visit the big havelis and share in their fireworks, but Ramu knew his family would be expecting him soon.

When he entered his house, Ramu closed his eyes. He wanted to be surprised. Munni and Ganga ran to him, each taking his hand. The sweet sandalwood incense filled the room and mingled with the heavy smell of jasmine. Ramu could hear his mother's anklets jingling and the rustling of her new sari.

'Open now!' squealed Munni and Ganga.

Ramu slowly opened his eyes. 'Aie-e-e-e.' He could say nothing more. There in a corner of the kitchen, in golden splendour, sat the Goddess Lakshmi, her four arms outstretched. In one hand she held the lotus flower from which she had sprung to life. In another hand she held a coin. In the third was the conch shell to blow upon. And her fourth hand was raised in a blessing. A red embroidered cloth, with two toy elephants and a toy mouse, was spread at the base of the statue. Jasmine garlands hung from Goddess Lakshmi's neck, and a plate of Diwali sweets rested on the altar before her.

'Touch nothing, beta,' cautioned his mother, 'until after you have bathed. Then we will make the offering.'

Ramu took the earthenware pot and went out into the courtyard. In the chill of the evening air he shivered as he poured the water over himself, and with extra care washed his face and hands and feet. How good it was a few minutes later to feel the heat of the room as he joined his family for the worship.

Kalu Ram led the evening prayers, after which each child put a silver coin at the feet of the Goddess. Now came the telling of Ramu's favourite story. This year Munni asked the important question.

'Bapuji,' she said, snuggling up to their father. 'What is Diwali?'

Kalu Ram put his arm around Munni, and the others drew closer together. The family sat on the floor and ate bits of coconut and sliced banana, as Kalu Ram began the story.

Long, long ago there ruled in the Kingdom of Ajodhya a king by the name of Dashrath. He was a good king and had ruled his people wisely. But when he grew old and tired and wished to retire, leaving the responsibilities of the kingdom to his most beloved son, Ram, a great tragedy befell the land.

You must know that during his reign King Dashrath had married three queens who had each borne him a son. Upon hearing the king's wishes, the third queen became angry and jealous. She wanted her son, Bharat, to sit on the throne instead of Ram. She was also a cunning woman and knew how to get her way. On one occasion, many years before, she had saved Dashrath's life, and in gratitude he had granted her two wishes.

Now the queen chose this very time to go before King Dashrath and demand her two boons. The first was that Prince Ram be banished to the forest for fourteen years. The second demand was that her son, Bharat, be crowned king immediately. When the old king heard these wishes, his heart broke. He pleaded with the queen to ask anything else and it would be granted. But the queen could not be swayed and only reminded him of his promise to her. If he did not grant these wishes, he would be guilty of breaking his word.

With great sorrow, the king called his son, Ram, to his side to give him the news. The gentle Ram did not think of himself but only of his father and how he might comfort him. His young wife, Seeta, and his devoted brother, Lakshman, pleaded to go into the forest with him.

And so it was. For fourteen years the three faced danger together, ate wild plant roots and berries, and slept under the stars.

But the jealous queen never got her second wish. For Bharat also loved his brother Ram and refused to be made king. Instead, he put the sandals of his brother on the throne and carried out the duties of the kingdom in his name.

'Children,' said Kalu Ram, 'Diwali is the day that Ram returned to his kingdom after fourteen years, and was crowned king. The people were mad with joy. Music played, candles were lit in every home, banners waved from every door and window, and the sky exploded into a rainbow of colour.'

'The *Ramayana* is the written story of this great king, and it has been the holy book of the Hindus throughout the ages. Ram ruled his people with strength and kindness. He had been an obedient son, a devoted brother, a loyal friend, and a brave soldier. All these qualities we try to live by. So, on this day every year, we rejoice and praise Ram.'

Kalu Ram had finished, but no one spoke. The wood in the fireplace crackled, and one by one the little flames in the earthen saucers reached the end of the wick and died out.

All at once Ganga jumped up as if stung by a bee. 'Ma! Bapuji! The presents. Where are the other presents?'

'Ah,' said Kalu Ram. 'I felt sure you would not forget, little mouse. They are in the storeroom. Run quickly.'

Ramu's heart began to pound. Was it possible? Had he been forgiven? Would one of the gifts be his mouth organ? He held his breath.

One present was opened, then another and another. The pile of newspaper in the middle of the circle grew. Ganga was knocking the ball with the bat, and Munni twirled her new bracelets. Ramu's hope sank. For the first time in his life he would not get a Diwali gift.

A knock sounded at the front door. While Kalu Ram went to open it, his wife covered her face with her sari. There in the open door stood Tulsi.

With folded hands he greeted Kalu Ram and said, 'I have come to see Ramu.'

Ramu hurried to his old friend and bent down to touch his feet.

'Ramu, beta, I have brought you a Diwali surprise,' explained Tulsi as he held out his hands. Cupped in his palms was a long, narrow object wrapped in coloured paper and tied with gay ribbons.

Ramu just stared.

'It is yours,' said Tulsi. 'It has always been yours.'

Ramu lowered his head. He felt the eyes of his family

burning into his back and knew what he must answer.

'I cannot take this gift, my friend. I have not earned
it.'

He put his forehead to Tulsi's feet and hoped he had
not hurt his friend's feelings. Yet how could he accept
with dishonour something he loved so much?

As he rose, Tulsi's eyes met his. They were warm and
understanding.

'Soon, beta,' he said, 'very soon it will be yours.'